The Lion Roars

written by Kathryn E. Lewis • illustrated by Susan Keeter

St. Clare of Montefalco School

Silver Burdett Ginn
A Division of Simon & Schuster
160 Gould Street
Needham Heights, MA 02194-2310

Design and production by BIG BLUE DOT

ISBN 0-663-59383-2

2 3 4 5 6 7 8 9 10 SP 01 00 99 98 97 96

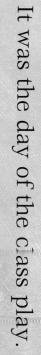

It was the day of the class play.

Matt was going to be a lion in the play.

Matt loved to say his lines again and again.
He loved to ROAR again and again.
He wanted his mom and dad to watch him
again and again.

So Matt looked for his mother.

"ROAR!" said Matt in a very loud voice.

"I am a brave lion. I live on the African plain.
I have a very long tail and a very large mane."

"Please, Matt, not now," his mother said.
"I have watched you many times.
I will watch you again in a little while."

Then Matt looked for his father.

"ROAR!" said Matt in a very loud voice.

"I am a brave lion. I live on the African plain.
I have a very long tail and a very large mane."

"Please, Matt, not now," his father said.
"I have watched you many times.
I will watch you again after your sister eats."

At last it was time for the play.

The class was ready.

Many people had come to see the play.

It was time for Matt to roar.

He looked at all the people.

All the people looked at him.

He tried to roar.
But not even a tiny
roar came out.

13

Just then Matt's sister saw him.

She stood up on her chair and waved.

"ROAR!" she shouted in a very loud voice.

Everyone smiled.
So did Matt.

"ROAR!" said Matt in a very loud voice.

"I am a brave lion. I live on the African plain.

I have a very long tail and a very large mane."